Return for Izzy

Penny

Penny

by Jane E. Gerver
Illustrated by Lisa Papp

SCHOLASTIC INC.

New York Toronto London Auckland Sydney
Mexico City New Delhi Hong Kong Buenos Aires

For Liz
– J. E. G.

For all children, who inherently know
good things come in small packages!
– L. P.

Library of Congress Cataloging-in-Publication Data

Gerver, Jane E.
Penny / by Jane E. Gerver ; illustrated by Lisa Papp.
p. cm. –– (Breyer stablemates)   "Cartwheel books."
Summary: To prove her worth as a potential queen, Princess Isabella and
her beloved pony Penny embark on a quest for twelve precious jewels.
ISBN 0-439-72235-7 (hardcover)
[1. Princesses--Fiction. 2. Ponies--Fiction. 3. Fairy tales.]
I. Papp, Lisa, ill. II. Title. III. Series.
PZ8.G3437Pen 2006   [E]--dc22   2005019155

12 11 10 9 8 7 6 5 4   7 8 9/0

Printed in China   62
First printing, July 2006

Table of Contents

The Test

It was the day of Princess Isabella's coronation. She would become the queen that night!

Everyone in the kingdom was busy.

They were cleaning, cooking, and planning a big parade.

But the princess was worried.

"What if I am not a good queen?"
Isabella asked her fairy godmother.

"If you pass the test, you will be," said
her fairy godmother. "Do not worry."

"What test?" asked Isabella.

Her fairy godmother handed her a scroll.

This is your quest:
Search trees, water, and sand.
Look for twelve jewels
Shiny and grand.

This is your test:
Be helpful, wise, and kind.
Then, as a true queen,
Your jeweled crown
you will find.

Isabella went to the royal stable. Which horse should she pick? The biggest? The fastest?

Then Isabella saw her beloved Shetland pony, Penny. Penny wasn't the fastest horse in the stable. And he wasn't the biggest. But he was the smartest of them all. And Isabella liked him the best!

The Enchanted Woods

Isabella saddled Penny and climbed onto his back. Penny trotted down the hill away from the castle and toward the forest

He and Isabella went into the Enchanted
Woods. The woods were dark and cool.
Penny had to walk slowly.

They did not see the crown anywhere. Soon they were lost among the trees. Which way should they go?

Isabella looked all around. Penny looked all around, too. He was hungry. He started to eat some leaves on a tree.

Just then, Isabella saw a baby bird on the ground.

"Oh, no!" Isabella said. "We have to help him!"

Isabella and Penny looked up into the tree and saw a nest. So Isabella got off of her pony. She picked up the baby bird.

Then she climbed onto Penny's back and stood up in her stirrups. Penny held very still. Isabella put the baby bird back into the nest. Then she noticed something shiny.

Three emeralds! She picked them out of
the nest. She jumped down to show them
to Penny. He whinnied. She put the emeralds
into Penny's saddlebags. Together they
rode out of the woods.

Shimmer River

The sun was warm. Soon it felt hot. Isabella was glad when they came to Shimmer River. Cold water rushed downstream. But there was no crown— and no bridge.

"We will have to ride across," the
princess said.

The rocks were slippery. Penny was
having trouble walking across them.

"Wait," Isabella said to Penny. "I will
walk, too, and it will be easier for you."

Isabella jumped down from Penny's back

Whoops! Splash! Isabella slipped and fell
into the river! But Penny was there.

He put his head into the water and
pulled Isabella out.

On the shore, Isabella hugged Penny.
"Thank you, my dear friend," she said.
Penny nuzzled her wet hair. Something
shiny fell out. It was a blue sapphire!

Penny nuzzled her hair again. Two more shiny sapphires dropped into her hands.

"Good work, Penny," Isabella said. "Now we only have to find six more jewels!"

Dusty Desert

The sun got hotter and hotter. Soon there was no shade at all.

"Look at all this sand!" the princess said. They had reached Dusty Desert.

Isabella and Penny were very thirsty. But there was no water to drink. Penny stopped at a cactus with red flowers. He whinnied loudly and stamped his hooves.

Isabella used her sword to open the cactus stem. Inside was water—and three shiny rubies! They were as red as the cactus flowers.

Isabella put the rubies in Penny's saddlebags. She shared the water with her pony.

"Good boy, Penny!" she said.

The Mountain

Penny and Isabella crossed the desert. They saw a large mountain ahead of them.

It was getting dark now. And it was very cold. Isabella saw a cave and rode up to it. She got off of Penny to look at it.

The cave was too small for Penny to enter.
Isabella was cold. She did not want to leave
Penny outside. But Penny didn't mind the
cold. He was fat and had a heavy coat. He
pushed Isabella into the cave with his nose.

Inside, Isabella looked around. She saw a
shiny spot on one wall. When she touched
it, three diamonds fell into her hands!
Suddenly, she heard a loud pop outside.
She stepped out of the cave.

Her fairy godmother stood near Penny,
holding a crown.

"May I please have the jewels, Isabella?"
asked her fairy godmother. Isabella gave
them to her fairy godmother, who placed
them in the crown.

"You passed the test, Isabella," said her
fairy godmother. "You were wise when you
picked Penny to join you on your quest.
You were helpful when you put the baby
bird back in its nest. And you were kind
when you got down from Penny's back to
cross the river. I know you will be a good
queen. Now it's time to go home."

The fairy godmother waved her hands.
POOF! At once, they were back at the
castle.

That night was the coronation.

Everyone cheered for the brave new queen
and her pony.

"Hooray for Queen Isabella!"

"Hooray for Penny!"

About the Pony

Photo: Bob Langrish, Gloucestershire, England

Facts on Shetlands:

1. Shetland ponies originally came from the Shetland Isles, off the coast of Scotland.

2. Of all the British pony breeds, Shetland ponies are the smallest, but they are very strong and sturdy.

3. The average Shetland pony is 10 hands or 40 inches tall. Horses are measured in "hands." A hand equals 4 inches.

4. Shetland ponies are very intelligent and can be used by children for riding and also for driving.

5. The American Shetland Pony Club was founded in 1890. The American Shetland pony is slightly larger and more refined than its British ancestors.